Eric Duncan

Rural Rhymes

and The sheep thief

Eric Duncan

Rural Rhymes
and The sheep thief

ISBN/EAN: 9783337260057

Printed in Europe, USA, Canada, Australia, Japan

Cover: Foto ©Andreas Hilbeck / pixelio.de

More available books at **www.hansebooks.com**

AND

THE SHEEP THIEF.

BY

ERIC DUNCAN.

TORONTO:

WILLIAM BRIGGS, WESLEY BUILDINGS.

C. W. COATES, Montreal, Que.   S. F. HUESTIS, Halifax, N.S.

1896.

These Rural Rhymes are not the rose-tinted reveries of a rusticating rhapsodist, but the regular, rough reminiscences of a real rancher, written by himself.

COMOX, BRITISH COLUMBIA,
    September, 1896.

CONTENTS.

RURAL RHYMES

A Mosquito Song.

Cow-HUNTING in the woods one day,
   I listened for the bell,
Holding my breath—when on my ear
   This song melodious fell.

" I am a bold mosquito,
    And through the woods I fly;
So get I but a drink of blood,
    I care not if I die.

" Creatures a thousand times as big
    Do bring my food to me;
I, singing, light astride on them,
    And grăb it out in glee!

" Yet though these creatures bring my food,
    Unwillingly they give,
And oft I find it hard to get
    The wherewithal to live.

" Great hairy brutes in companies
　　Will sluggishly draw near ;
　Their hides are all so thick and tough
　　They well-nigh break my spear.

" And when I get a drop of blood,
　　It is not worth the pains—
　Coarse, salt, and indigestible,
　　It on my chest remains.

" But there is one, a monster dire,
　　Who sometimes passes by
　(Oh, had I but my fill of blood,
　　I satisfied would die !).

"To light upon this monster dire　.
　　Is risk of life and limb ;
　But I would risk a hundred lives
　　To get a sip from him.

" His hide is thin, his blood is sweet—
　　Sweeter than milk to me ;
　But ah, his ways are full of guile,
　　And treacherous is he !

" At times he like a stump will stand,
　　And you would think him dead,
　Then suddenly he wakes, and flails
　　Go thrashing round his head.

" Oh, I have seen—have seen—have seen "—
    (He hovered as he sang)
" Five comrades flattened at my side
    Beneath one frightful bang!

" But I, a bold mosquito,
    Still through the forest fly,
And I will have a drink of blood,
    I care not though I die."

———

Here ceased the song, for, with a slap,
    The singer bold I slew.
See, ye whose love for liquor grows,
    What it may do for you.

An Ox Song.

I HAVE an ox, a good work ox,
　　Steady to plough or draw;
Not vicious he, his only fault
　　Is kleptomania.

He has a long and lanky frame,
　　His belly nought can fill,
Yea, should he gulp a bale of hay
　　He would be lanky still.

Beside his elephantine height
　　An eight-rail fence is low;
He hugs the fence, he reaches down
　　Where high the oats do grow.

A taste—a bite—he lifts his head;
　　Now run!—and yell!—and run!—
Too late!　His ponderous bulk upheaves,
　　And crash! the work is done.

One dawn I found him trampling through
　　My heaviest field of grain;
All night he had been toiling there
　　To fill himself—in vain.

I tied him to the broken fence,
　A crab-tree switch I tore
(For I was mad), and thrashed him as
　He ne'er was thrashed before.

He took it all full patiently,
　He knew it was his due,
But yet at me, when loosing him,
　A spiteful look he threw—

A look which said, as plain as speech,
　"My hide is disarranged,
Oh-h-h! but I will remember this,
　And I will be revenged."

Next night when I in peaceful bunk
　Did comfortably snore,
Roused by a raging storm of bells,
　I sprang upon the floor.

"Much good one sinner doth destroy,"
　Said the wise king of old;
The words came forcibly as I
　A blanket round me rolled.

No time for socks, I quickly plunged
　Barefoot into my boots,
And, lighted by the round-faced moon,
　Sped fast through brush and roots.

Oho! they fill the turnip field,
　Cows gobbling all they can;
But see the huge, ungainly form
　That lumbers in their van!

The moon, the calm, indifferent moon,
　My frenzied fury mocks,
As round and round the field I tear
　After that dreadful ox.

I cleared the place, but not before
　The crop was half destroyed;
Now many a night-alarm have I,
　And many an hour employed

In mending gaps, for though no more
　That ox will wander free,
The cows, through his example, are
　Almost as bad as he.

But I have seen the foolishness
　Of trifling with a thief,
And so this good but erring ox
　Will very soon be beef.

𝔄 Cow Song.

SUMMER finds the Comox farmer
    Work enough to do ;
Labor-bent, he ceaseless trudges,
    Like the mythic Jew.

Does he slacken ? Weeds in turnips,
    Fern among the grain,
Outspread hay, and dark clouds gathering,
    Spur him on again.

Crafty pigs and steers and horses,
    Shrewd fence-breakers all,
Send him over heights of madness
    Nigh beyond recall.

But the last big straw which fractures
    His devoted back,
Is the brute that gives the bucket
    Its despatching whack.

Ah, what grins distend her nostrils !
    Ah, what eyes of mirth !
As the white flood leaps, and mingles
    With the thirsty earth !

Listen while I tell the story,
    As it haunts me now,
Of a farmer's sad adventure
    With a kicking cow.

———

Starting up before the sunrise,
    Flushed the brow of morn,
He had brushed the soaking dew-drops
    From the fern and thorn,

Gathering in his cows to milk them
    Ere resistless beams
Pierced through cool green shades, and wakened
    Gadflies from their dreams.

Twos and threes he found, and turned them
    On the homeward road,
Till at length, amid the roughland,
    Only one abode.

She, of all the herd the leader,
    Ever wandered far,
Far into the darkest forest
    Where the cedars are.

So he left her, and she came not
    Till meridian rays
Filled with breathless heat the valley
    And a shimmering haze.

Oh, the sun was fiercely burning;
    Thick the air, and still;
Not a bird note—every raven
    Gasped with gaping bill.

In the pond the swine were rolling;
    Rover panting lay;
But above and all around them
    Gadflies boomed away.

Through the sultry lanes of woodland
    Rang the wanderer's song,
As in lonesome haste she hurried
    Desperately along.

Swooped upon by flying squadrons,
    Furiously she bounds,
Lashing vengeful tail, and bleeding
    From a hundred wounds.

Right into the shed she darted,
    Through the open door,
And a weary smile of welcome
    Her tired owner wore.

Tight he closed the door and screened her
    From the scorching day,
Yet a stealthy native entered
    With his assegai.

    *   *   *   *   *

On his one-legged stool, so busy
　　As the farmer sat,
Suddenly, like ball at cricket
　　Spinning from a bat,

From between his knees the bucket
　　Banged against the wall,
And what little milk was in it
　　Showered around the stall.

Then he took a piece of bale rope,
　　And, with many a turn,
To the stall and to a wall-post
　　Moored her, stem and stern.

" Now," said he, " my lady Fidget,
　　Do the worst you can ;"
And again, with steady cadence,
　　Fast the white streams ran.

Patiently she stood, in silent
　　Meditation wrapt,
Till the heavy pail was brimming,
　　Then—the sisal snapt.

Rampant overhead, her dewlaps
　　On his shoulders come ;
Prone he falls, and, grovelling, wallows
　　In the seething foam !

And she grimly smiled—and vanished
　　From his wildered view,
Squarely through the door so slender,
　　Like a bomb she flew.

A Bull Song.

I.

JUST here the river bounds
　　The cultivated ground ;
Far stretches, on the other shore,
　　The wilderness profound.

Where Tsolum rolls his waves
　　Through woods of spruce and pine,
And mighty cottonwoods their boughs
　　With maples intertwine;

Where giant trunks of eld,
　　In mossy ridges flung,
Wallow in white-thorn, dogwood, crab,
　　With brambles overstrung;

Where far-extending sloughs,
   And paths without an end,
Run through the tangling undergrowth
   With many a wildering bend ;

In this enchanting land,
   This country of the coon,
Free cattle multitudinous
   Spend every circling June.

Right opposite there dwelt,
   In thrall and discontent,
A sturdy bull, which longed to break
   From his enforced restraint.

Still daily as he came
   Returning thirst to slake,
Free rovers, on the other side,
   Would jeer him from the brake.

At last an ancient foe
   One evening vaunting spoke,
And ring and chain were all in vain—
   Across the surge he broke.

And now, from bondage free,
   Exultingly he sang ;
The live-long night his trumpet tones
   Through the dark forest rang.

II.

O! music rode the breeze
   That night through Comox groves,
As bull-frog, owl, and bull combined
   To serenade their loves!

O! tenor sang the frog,
   And bass the night-bird lone,
But high above them swelled and rolled
   The bull's grand baritone.

Vain exultation his;
   The sun's first rising beam
Next morning saw a rancher bold
   Breasting the bridgeless stream.

Through many a tortuous trail,
   Through many a slough forlorn,
He tracked him to a scrubby height
   By fire of timber shorn.

Whizz through the thickets flew
   The wild herd o'er the hill;
Less fleet, less scared, the bull remains;
   High peals his war-note shrill.

Heedless of hostile show
　　The rancher heads him home ;
Sullen and slow he walks till to
　　The river's bank they come.

Then blazed his ire, to view
　　Afar his den of woe ;
With flaming eyes he turned and drove
　　Headlong against the foe.

The rancher stept aside
　　From swift destruction's path ;
A club upon the flying death
　　He splintered in his wrath.

Back through the serpent track,
　　Back with green slime bedight,
Back with a rush that ne'er did slack,
　　Back o'er the bushy height ;

Joins the wild herd again,
　　The rancher close behind,
Lashed by rebounding twigs, and slashed
　　By thorns with briers twined.

Yet with endurance strong
　　He rounds them up once more,
Singles the bull, and riverward
　　Again they madly tore.

Dash through the scrubby pines,
  Splash through the sweltering slough,
Crash over logs with brambles bound,
  And dead snags jutting through ;

On through the opening brakes,
  On to the Tsolum's bound,
Each thundering footfall jars and shakes
  The root-cemented ground.

Fagged the stout brute at last ;
  Foam-streaked his heaving sides ;
He reached the bank and rolled into
  The cool, refreshing tides.

Cowed and disheartened, he
  Submitted like a lamb ;
Upon his back his captor leapt,
  And o'er the flood he swam.

———

Thus the poor bovine king
  For freedom fought in vain,
And with the shades of night returned
  To his detested chain.

A Hog Song.

I.

In the days that are departed
  Lived the subject of my song,
When these limbs, now old and feeble,
  Were with youthful vigour strong.

Long ere Vernon,* foe to grunters,
  Rose to curb their liberty,
'Midst the ferns and swamps of Comox
  Mighty swine dwelt joyously.

From the marking time and onward
  To the dreadful slaughter day,
Through the woods, and o'er the prairies,
  At their pleasure wandered they.

Grim old boars, with tusks ferocious,
  Drove the skulking panther back ;
In a bristling ring they marshalled,
  And defied the wolves' attack.

Ah, those days forever vanished !
  Ah, those years so wild and free !
Ere great Vernon, foe to grunters,
  Robbed them of their liberty.

*   *   *   *   *   *

* Vernon was the author of the Provincial Act prohibiting
swine from running at large.

One bright morning in November
   Often through my mind doth run,
When the brown fern, white with hoar frost,
   Shone like silver in the sun.

Done the digging of potatoes,
   And the turnip pulling too;
I was standing in my doorway
   Thinking what I next should do.

When from out the leafy margin
   Of the woodland stalked along,
Toward the log-hut snug and solid
   Where he used to sleep when young,

An old hog, of vast proportions,
   Lost to sight for many a day,
Dark and fierce as night and tempest,
   With his bristles turning gray.

As it chanced, the door was fastened,
   But he lingered, and a whim—
Reasonless, absurd—possessed me,
   All alone to capture him.

Soon he passed behind the cabin,
   Where some berry bushes grew,
Hiding me and every movement
   Altogether from his view.

Straight a train of turnip slices
　　Laid I, stretching far afield
From the sty's now open doorway ;
　　Quickly then myself concealed.

Muttering to himself, and grumbling,
　　Now the hog again appeared ;
When he saw the line of turnips,
　　Ears and bristles both upreared.

Plainly he a trick suspected,
　　For he sniffed but would not taste,
And towards the sheltering forest
　　Turned, as to retreat in haste.

But a stray slice came before him,
　　And he snatched it.　Ah, the lack
In his stomach overcame him ;
　　All his youth came rushing back.

Back he turned and swallowed, smacking,
　　And his head he raised no more
Till the open sty received him,
　　And I slammed the heavy door.

With a beam I barred it, mortised
　　Into logs on either side,
And I heaped great stones against it ;
　　" Now I have you safe ! " I cried.

II.

To a hole high in the gable
   Mounting, I looked down within,
And the captive, glancing upward,
   Welcomed me with savage grin.

Then he gnashed his teeth in fury,
   And his eyes gleamed luridly,
As he spoke in grim defiance—
   "Guff! guff! ugh!" he snarled at me.

Undismayed I dropt beside him,
   Seized him firmly by the tail.
To describe the scene that followed,
   Words all miserably fail.

With ear-splitting yells he circled
   Round and round at dizzying pace,
While each vain attempt to check him
   Only spurred him in his race.

Round my arm a rope coil fastened
   Loosened, tripped me, and anon
Flat as flounder on the sty floor
   I was thrown, yet hung I on.

Plunging, kicking, twisting, shrieking,
   Fast and thick he gasped at last,
Then in one grand break for freedom
   His remaining strength he cast.

As a battering-ram of old time,
   Forward dashed, with shattering blow,
Broke beleaguered gates, and hurled them
   Down in awful overthrow,

So, with bound of desperation,
   He his headlong passage tore,
Crashing through the solid planking
   Of the barricaded door.

Bars and barriers flew before him—
   Rocks in vain obstruct the way—
Tattered, bruised, yet hanging to him
   Out upon the field I lay.

Then he turned upon me, shaking,
   Breathless, streaked with foam he was ;
But he only ripped my boot leg
   Ere he loosed his quivering jaws ;

For a dreadful kick I planted
   Right above his fiery eyes,
Stars by thousands danced before him,
   And he fell, no more to rise.

Well may you believe that quickly
  Hues of scarlet dyed the ground
As the savage blood in torrents
  Issued from a deadly wound.

Ah ! but he is long departed ;
  Of his race the few that be,
Rugged-backed and chicken-hearted
  Wail their vanished liberty.

A January Song.

WINTER, tyrant stern and hoary,
　　Rules with iron sway the fields;
Over wrecks of Autumn's glory
　　Glittering monuments he builds.
Whistles sharp his minion Boreas,
　　Galvanized at his advance;
Dead leaves leap and whirl before us
　　Through the woods in ghostly dance.

Skies, grey-ribbed and frost-corroded,
　　Smooth and thicken like a pall,
Bending low, and overloaded,
　　Down they let their burden fall.
Tumbling, scattering, flickering, flying,
　　Come the flakes in headlong haste,
While an aimless wind is sighing
　　Drearily from waste to waste.

Animated nature shivers,
　　Stricken through with deadly chill;
Buried are the ponds and rivers,
　　Shrouded every bush-topped hill.

O for March's roaring bluster !
  O for April's drizzling rain !
Yea, we hail even thee, South-easter,
  See we but green earth again.

*   *   *   *   *   *

Unperceived the sun is passing
  O'er the glacier peak afar,
Sombre clouds, behind him massing,
  Herald the approaching war,
When, like resurrected giant,
  Bursts the gale Chinookian forth,
And with ringing blast defiant,
  Sweeps the routed Winter north.

*   *   *   *   *   *

As upon the desolation
  Of the dead lands, sunk in snow,
Life shoots up, a new creation,
  As the great South-easters blow,
So when, prosperous times forsaking,
  Adverse fortunes o'er us roll,
Aye, through chilling glooms forth-breaking,
  Hope revivifies the soul.

Deep within the breast implanted,
  Hope, the offspring of the sky,

Bowed by storms, yet springs undaunted ;
    Ice-encased, it cannot die.
By it still, through crime and sorrow,
    Doomed unfortunates are blest ;
Still, against the doubtful morrow,
    Each one is an optimist.

Go, with God acknowledged near you,
    While fair sunshine floods your way,
Hope perennial then will cheer you
    In the dark and cloudy day ;
Till, earth's shadows thinning, rending,
    Breaks upon your strengthened sight
All the Summer joy unending
    Of the land of fadeless light.

𝔄 𝔐ay 𝔖ong.

Written on the occasion of the Nanaimo colliery explosion of 1887, the
greatest disaster in the history of British Columbia.]

CAN this indeed be May,
　　That month so green and fair ?
Surely November at its worst
　　Could scarce with this compare.

Huge clouds of blackest hue
　　In dense battalions form,
And trees uproot, and fences fly,
　　Before the warring storm.

The shivering cows rush home
　　To shun the fierce downpour,
And ancient straw and musty hay
　　They eagerly devour.

The brimming river foams,
　　With current brown and strong,
And over ploughed and seeded lands
　　The wild duck sails along.

　　*　　*　　*　　*　　*　　*

But these are trifles.   Ah !
 What real trouble springs
Where Death's dark angel hovers low,
 With close and stifling wings !

Woe for the stricken town !
 Woe for the homes of gloom,
Which husband, son, or father's face
 Shall never more illume !

Oh, month of cloud and wrath !
 Long, long, through future years
Nanaimo will remember thee
 With sighing and with tears.

God bind the broken hearts,
 God comfort those who mourn,
For what can human aid avail
 In such a time forlorn ?

A June Song.

Now clouds are wearing thin,
   Now verdure wraps the land
From the high snow's receding bound
   Down to the Georgian strand.

The sun benignly smiles—
   Not yet his might he wields,
Nor frowns with fiery countenance
   Upon the fainting fields.

And breezes rustle by,
   And bells ring through the woods,
And bird-notes ever merrily
   Fill up the interludes.

Swallows through empty barns
   Dart swift, on tireless wing,
And underneath the rafters high
   Their nests are fashioning.

The river's shrinking tide
   Leaves snags and beaches dry ;
With headlong rush, 'twixt wave and air
   Young ducks athwart it fly.

Now lifts the fern his head
    Above the growing grain—
Undying foe, oft smitten down,
    But bound to rise again.

Wily and powerful he,
    Who would with him contend
In vigilance must tireless be,
    And fight him to the end.

Yet perfume of the rose,
    With scent of clover blends,
And warm and soft, with soundless fall,
    The summer snow descends.*

Far upward we have climbed
    From depths of winter drear;
Now hail we thee, O glorious June,
    The summit of the year

---

* The down of the great cottonwood tree, which often
falls as thick as a shower of snow.

A July Song.

O, BLAZINGLY hot are these days of July,
　Down here in this dale of the West!
Not a breeze in the trees, not a cloud in the sky,
　Not a break on the bay's calm breast.
O how fine it would be in the shadow to lie,
Where the pine throws his wide-spreading branches on
　　　high;
But mosquitoes and gadflies hum rousingly by,
. And July is no time for rest.

Weeds, weeds must be slain, and the hay mown down,
　Tossed, raked, cocked, and pitched on the wain;
And all must be done 'neath the sun's fierce frown,
　While the sweat pours down like rain.
Ye who talk of the smoke and the heat of the town,
And for sweet-smelling clover do hunger and groan,
If yoked but a day to the hay-field so brown,
　You would wish for your desks again.

Drought.

AUGUST returns, but not with plenty crowned;
　　Thin, dwarfed, and light of head is all the grain.
The meagre hay was, ere its blossom, browned;
　　The root crops withered, all for want of rain.
The cows for aftergrass do seek in vain,
　　And through the boundless woods afar they roam.
They anger me; but when driven home again
　　Their sad eyes plead for hay, and I am dumb,
For I have none to spare—I think of months to come.

A November Song.

WILD sweeps the dark South-easter by, in torrents falls
    the rain,
The Tsolum overflows his banks and inundates the plain ;
Upon his yellow current borne, with many a crash and
    groan,
Great spars, and ragged trunks of trees torn from the
    roots, drive on.
The salmon leave the turbid flood, no more their highway
    now,
And byways take through field and wood where tiniest
    streamlets flow.
Though endless barriers block their course, they circum-
    vent them all—
The log, the rock, the gravelly bar, the tumbling waterfall.
Mile after mile they leap and creep, nor of returning think,
While water wets their tails, or they can find a drop to
    drink.*

The geese, in solid wedge-like ranks, well-ordered, south
    have passed,
And ducks and cranes in wavering lines now ride the
    surly blast.

---

* The British Columbia salmon might almost be classed among the amphibia.
Only an eye-witness can credit the extent of his inland journeyings.

The yards where herds do congregate are ankle-deep in
    mire,
And long-legged boots and overcoats we farmers all require.

Gone are the sunny summer days, the harvest glory lost,
The wretched earth is wearied by alternate rain and frost;
The maple's gorgeous garb is now a scanty veil of brown,
And from their June-time refuge high the snows are
    edging down.*
But yet, though greybeard Winter comes, he brings with
    him along
The cheerful round of fireside joys, the reading and the
    song.
Who will may seek the crowded town, or range the stormy
    sea,
This quiet, independent life is just the life for me.

---

* The central ridge of Vancouver Island is always snow-capped.

An Elegy.

He who rose and roused his household
    In the dawning grey,
Rises not, nor lifts an eyelid,
    All the sunny day.

He who brought the cows from pasture
    Ere the sun grew hot,
At the gate they wait, and wonder
    Why they see him not.

He, the ever-foremost mower
    In the hayfield blithe,
Suddenly is struck, and levelled
    By a mightier scythe.

And that ringing shout which answered
    Aye the noontide horn,
Rings no more, nor faintest whisper
    Cheers the home forlorn.

Stilled the voice that led in worship,
    Sure as evening fell ;
Younger hands must take the Bible
    That he loved so well.

*   *   *   *   *   *

Sturdily his path of labor
    To the end he trod ;
Lay him, worn, not rust-corroded,
    Underneath the sod.

Weedroots, longtime fought, may quickly
    Bind each rugged hand ;
What recks he ? a restful dweller
    In the weedless Land.

THE SHEEP THIEF.

A LEGEND OF SHETLAND.

From that dark shore full many a league removed,
  'Neath summer skies, 'mid milder scenes I roam,
Yet never from my mind, O land beloved !
  Thy image fades, my boyhood's happy home.
  A hemisphere of land and stormy foam
Divides me from thee, yet, for evermore,
  Thy green and daisied fields before me come,
Thy sombre hills, thy headlands huge and hoar,
And white waves surging on, with far-resounding roar.

THE SHEEP THIEF.

PART I

AWAY beneath the northern sky
The rugged Isles of Shetland lie ;
Land of the Vikings, who of yore
Ravaged each neighboring sea and shore,
And oft, in battle fierce, defied
The Danish and the Saxon pride.
Their day is gone, their power is vain,
Yet cliffs and caves their names retain.
And still, as in that age afar,
The ocean's everlasting war
Rages around their bulwarked home,
With futile wrath and frantic foam.

There rises, on the western coast,
Where beat Atlantic storms the most,
A giant cliff—a dizzy height—
Ascending far beyond the might
Of wildest waves. Thorsfjeld its name,
From the strong god of hammer fame.

THE SHEEP THIEF.

It seems a mountain cleft in twain,
The landward slopes alone remain :
Sheer from the summit to the sea
It stoops, in grey immensity.

Full thirty yards adown the steep,
Behind a ledge where ravens sleep,
   Still may the sailor mark,
Rent in the rock, an aperture
Low browed and wide, a fitting door
   To cavern rude and dark.
The cragsman's eye has never seen
   The secrets of that cavern deep ;
The cragsman's foot has never been
   Upon that ledge where ravens sleep.
Swung in mid-air, he eyes in vain
   That door and shelf of rock :
O'erhanging crags their guard maintain.
Seaward he springs, a hold to gain ;
The rocks his inward sway restrain,
   And all his efforts mock.*

Here dwelt, the old traditions say,
What time the Isles owned Norway's sway,
   A Being strange and strong.
With deep-set eyes of lurid cast,

* See Note I.

Of stature low, with shoulders vast,
The disproportioned creature passed
  All noiselessly along,
Frightening the carle at closing eve,
Who in his heart did well believe
He saw a Trow of nether earth,
And not a man of mortal birth.

His clothing was the skins of sheep
Which wandered near his stronghold steep.
A stout crook-headed iron rod,
Rounded and pointed like a goad,
For weapon in his hand he bore ;
And so was called, the country o'er,
From Fitful Head to Nordenhaff,
The Sheep Thief with the iron staff.

Now, how he did contrive to climb,
Or how descend, that height sublime,
Without a rope, companionless,
Men oft would speculate and guess.
His long arms for the crags seemed made,
And probably his staff did aid.
Indeed, a certain Hakon Gyar
Some awe and wonder did inspire
By telling how, when in his skiff,
One calm dark night below the cliff

He saw a smoky brightness start
Forth from the cave, and upward dart,
Which, as the mountain top it struck,
The form of horse and rider took.
And this, he said, did clearly show
That Tangie* bore him to and fro.
But Gyar was of romancing vein,
And credence small his tale did gain ;
And to the dwarf, 'twas thought, alone
Some subterranean way was known,
Opening on Thorsfjeld's eastern combe,
Through which he brought his plunder home.

Sad havoc in the flocks he made
That through the Thorsfjeld country strayed.
His nightly frolics were, to creep,
In their own garments, to the sheep,
Then suddenly upon them rise,
And break their legs, or pierce their eyes
With his staff point.   It was his joy
To torture, mangle, and destroy.
As fast as any dog he ran,
Outstripping far the swiftest man ;
Ay, even men began to fear
Singly to range the region there,
For late, a shepherd from that place
Had disappeared, without a trace.

* See Note II.

In all Dunrossness there was not
    A man like Ola Brand,
Great Sumburgh's stoutest son was but
    A stripling in his hand.
A giant he, in height and build,
The huge war-axe which he did wield
Was known on many a bloody field
    Within the southern land.
And he could take a galley's chain
And snap it with a jerk in twain,
    Like straw-rope, easily.
Barehanded he a bull had foiled ;
Amazed, the charging brute recoiled,
To find himself of horns despoiled,
    As Brand walked idly by.
Brown moorland, hill, and sheltered glen,
From Thofsfjeld east to Levenden,
And north from Quendal's sandy bay
To the great hill of Halaleigh,
St. Ringan's Isle, and Westerskord,
All owned him for their Udal lord.

Hundreds of light-brown sheep* had he,
Which pastured on the grassy lea

---

* These light-brown, or "moorad" sheep are a breed
peculiar to the Isles, and their wool is of special value.

Of Thorsfjeld, and his tenants all
Had sheep in heathery Westerdahl ;
And every year they lost their best
By this wild plunderer of the West.
But now the bounds of suff'rance tame
Were past, when o'er the hills there came
To Ola, on a summer noon,
The tidings of his shepherd gone.

No word he spake of bad or good,
But straight to Thorsfjeld took his road.
Hills, moory wastes, before him lay ;
He reached the height ere close of day.
Upon a rock he took his seat,
And waited there the Thief to meet,
    While soft the evening fell,
And limitless to the north-west
The placid ocean heaved its breast
    With slow majestic swell.
That fateful sea, that solemn sea
Which wraps the Pole of mystery,
And over which, in that old day,
Still sailed his countrymen away,
West-bound for Greenland's barren shore,
Or dreary coasts of Labrador
(Future as yet the Genoese
With all his grand discoveries).

The sun was passing to his bed
Through amber halls with curtains red,
  Beyond the northern haze ;
And lo ! behind, a shining bridge
Spanned each long undulating ridge
Of swell, connecting with the ledge
  Northward from Thorsfjeld's base,
Like causeway leading from its edge
  To endless polar days.
And every smooth-backed skerry-rock,
Each cape that braves the tempest shock,
And each fantastic pillared block
  Glowed in the sea of fire.
One vast and isolated stone
Rose like a king of ages gone:
Around his head a golden zone,
  And purple his attire ;
While, breaking o'er his feet and throne,
The wavelets sparkled, danced, and shone
  Like rubies and sapphire.

What is that hollow sound so deep?
The tides which through the Dorholm sweep
  With melancholy wail ;
That ocean door through which a ship
  Might run with swelling sail ;

4

While overhead the mighty arc
Of rough grey stone, like skin of shark,
And underneath the surges dark
    Echo the shrieking gale.

Myriads of gulls upon the rocks,
Puffins, and guillemots, and auks,
    And "skarfs" upon the sea,
High eagles, circling in the blue,
And the Norse birds of sombre hue,*
Intent their various aims pursue,
    And scream incessantly.

Black to the north, Old Rona rose
Across the intervening voes ;
His granite shoulders scarred with "gylls,"
The highest peak in all the Isles ;
Far to the west, where sea and sky
Meet, merge, and mingle mistily,
Like pale blue clouds arising, stand
The mural heights of Foula-land.

Then sank the lingering sun to rest,
Flew every sea-bird to its nest,
And the grey "dimm" from ocean's breast
    Rose silently aloft;

----
* Ravens.

Enwrapping crag and columned stone,
It filled with ghosts the region lone,
Their shrouds and draperies all its own,
   Waved by the night breeze soft.
Yet still on Rona's giant head
The day's departing beam was shed;
That peak reflects a glimmering light
Through all the short-lived summer night.

So changed the scene, with dying day,
Its glorious hues for sober grey;
Deep silence settled all around,
Save for the Dorholm's slumbrous sound.
But on that rampart of the land
Still sat and waited Ola Brand.

Hark, was not that a stealthy tread?
The watcher quickly turned his head,
When, swift from out the spectral "dimm,"
A shapeless form advanced to him.
Like lightning from his seat he sprang;
At once upon the boulder rang
The clangour of the iron staff.
"Aha!" cried Brand, with scornful laugh;
And ere the dwarf regained his sway,
He seized and wrenched the bar away.

Out through the dark it whizzed and spun
Like fiery meteor, and was gone.

Then Brand (his lordly form upreared
To its full height) vainglorious jeered
    His little enemy :
" Although I cannot strike a blow
With such as thou, yet deign to know
Thy staff is gone where thou wilt go
    To bear it company."
Sudden he ceased, for with a bound
The dwarf was at him, and around
    His body quick had cast
His long lithe arms, like steely bands,
And pinioned to his sides his hands,
    And held him tight and fast.

As northern hunter, in the grasp
    Of bear, on icy field,
Strains every nerve, with choking gasp,
While slowly 'neath the mighty clasp
    His ribs begin to yield ;
So Ola, in the stern embrace
Of that weird Being, for a space
    Did struggle fruitlessly.
And landward now their course they urge,
Now to the mountain's utmost verge,

Above the quiet sea.
As to the precipice they swung,
With desperate strength, all torn and wrung
   One hand did Ola free;
And by the neck he clutched the dwarf,
As cragsman grasps the sentry "skarf".*
   A fearful hold took he.
Like as a sponge in flood that swims,
When squeezed, spouts forth its copious streams,
So, forced by that gigantic grip,
Flew the black blood from nose and lip
Of the fell Thief, who slacked his hold,
And, hurled upon the greensward, rolled
Insensate. His rash foe, as well,
Spent, breathless, almost fainting, fell.

Powerless for ill, they lay a space,
When all at once a thundering pace
Startled the stillness of the place,
   And, ringing in their ears,
Roused e'en the Thief! Far down the side
Where Thorsfjeld melts in moorland wide,
Clearing a rod at every stride,
   A wondrous horse appears.
As black as coal that horse did seem,
Straight as an arrow-flight he came,

---

* See Note III.

His eyes and nostrils flashing flame,
　　Which flared above his head ;
He mounts the mountain at a breath,
As springs blue lightning over heath ;
Up blazed the grass beside his path,
　　And fell in ashes dead !
He scales the crest, a moment halts,
Then terror first Brand's soul assaults.
But lo ! the Thief upon him vaults,
　　And o'er the cliff they flew.
"No liar, then, was Hakon Gyar,"
Said Brand, betwixt dismay and ire.
"The wretch is leagued with demons dire,
　　And what can mortal do ?"

As, baffled, now he seeks his home,
Behold ! a lessening of the gloom.
Sudden the glimmer which had crept
All night along the North Sea, leapt
Aloft into the grey, and sprays
Of green and gold, and purple rays
Blended with rose-hues, following fast,
O'er the dim waves a radiance cast.
Rona's majestic summit flamed,
And many a lesser ward-hill beamed.
At Ola's feet on Thorsfjeld crest
Up springs a laverock from its nest,

To raise on high the morning song
Which fellow-choristers prolong.
The bright north-east still brighter glows,
Each night-born shadow fainter grows,
Till in full blaze of summer light
The glorious sun bursts on the sight.

PART II.

The days pass on.   The summer dies ;
On wings the Shetland autumn flies ;
Low in the south the sun's pale ball
Contends with clouds, which conquer all.
Bleak winds across the moorlands roar ;
Thunder the waves along the shore.
On Rona's peak and Halaleigh
The early snows lie, scant and grey.
A six-hours' day !   Winter has come ;
Now is the sky a leaden dome,
While tossed and fanned by Boreas old,
The cloud-chaff sweeps o'er hill and wold.

One dark December morn, when wind
And drifting snow their might combined,
And over naked land and sea
Ruled with unbridled tyranny.

Within the house of Ola Brand
His servants all assembléd stand.
They meet to search the wilds for sheep
Beneath the snowdrifts buried deep,
In glens, and dahls, and skords, and gylls,*
Upon the lee-sides of the hills.

"Do ye," said Ola to the men,
"Hold northward over Levenden,
The slopes of Halaleigh ascend,
And westward thence your course must tend
Across the wastes to Westerdahl,
Scouring the glens and passes all.
To Thorsfjeld I will take my course—
Ye fear the Thief and Demon-horse ;
But ne'er must it be said that I
From man or fiend did flinch or fly."

Then speedily the peasants shared
The digging implements prepared,
And forth upon their quest they fared
    Into the blinding grey.
And soon the stoutest of the throng
Of Ola's ponies, staunch and strong,†

---

* "Skords and gylls"—gorges and ravines.
† See Note IV.

Hair black and shaggy, thick and long,
  His master bore away.
Along the stormy ridges swept
Clean bare, the watchful Northman kept,
Though oft perforce the pony leapt
  O'er hollows full of snow.
Fierce growled the blast, with growing wrath,
In eddying gusts around their path ;
They held the course with laboring breath,
  They scarce could see to go.

So passed they on, o'er moor and bog,
Till, dimly through the rushing fog,
  The bulk of Thorsfjeld loomed ;
And high above the windy jar
Rose the deep tones of ocean's war,
As through the Dorholm arch afar
  The billows rolled and boomed.
The Thorsfjeld glens traversing round,
With care did Ola search and sound,
And many a buried flock he found,
  Some dead, but most alive ;
For those small sheep are brave and stout,
The wintry storms they weather out ;
Roaming the treeless wilds about,
  On heather shoots they thrive.

And Shetland snows are quickly gone,
By furious sea-gales overblown.

The mountain slopes he thus explored
Northward, to where the surges roared,
When, rounding a projecting rock,
The pony swerved, with sudden shock,
And there the Thief before them stood,
His right hand grasped his iron rod
(The selfsame bar by Ola sent
Far through the summer firmament),
A struggling sheep was in his left,
Whose skull a recent blow had cleft.

Dropping his prey, with blackest scowl,
He raised his bolt and with a howl
At Ola sprang, whose iron hand   .
Received the blow, but took command
Of the grim weapon.   Whirled on high,
The Dwarf still clung tenaciously,
Till dashed to earth, the horse's feet
Made his discomfiture complete.

Not thus might that dark life be sped ;
Instant he writhed him free and fled
Staffless.   He seemed to fly as fast
As if with wings, before the blast,

Heading where winds and waters rave
Around the cliff that guards his cave.

Fast in pursuit did Ola come,
Urging his pony through the gloom,
Though scarce the sturdy beast had need
Of hand or voice to quicken speed ;
And many a rough ravine they crossed,
But soon the fleeing shape was lost—
Enveloped in the murky white,
Away it passed beyond their sight.

They reached a "gyll" both wide and deep ;
Endless its length, its sides were steep,
   And drifted soft below.
The pony rose in headlong leap ;
He touched, but footing could not keep,
And man and horse, all in a heap,
   Rolled back into the snow.
Quickly arising, Brand espied
A horse upon the farther side,
   And, in the gully broad
Deep sunk, he left his own to wait
Till he returned, or extricate
His wallowing bulk alone, by fate
   The Stranger he bestrode.

With arrowy speed the Stranger flew
Away, away; the path he knew,
   Up Thorsfjeld's mighty breast;
And hot his body seemed to grow
To Ola's touch, and flakes of snow
Fizzed on his hide, and made no show;
   And ever on he pressed
Till, as he reached the topmost height,
Beneath his feet the frosty white
   Did blacken, melt, and hiss.
Fire from his eyes and nostrils sprung,
And back to earth the Northman flung
Himself, as out the Demon swung
   Into the wild abyss!

Then, as he crouched upon the verge,
Shriek upon shriek rose o'er the surge—
   Dreadful unearthly cries.
The shuddering giant feebly crawled
Close to the brink, and shrank appalled.
   Far down the precipice,
Dim, as the spray-clouds swept aside
A space, the Outlaw he descried,
Clinging, with aspect horrified,
   Above his cavern door;
While close beside, on sable wing,
The Demon-horse was hovering.

Not timely succor now to bring;
  No, furiously he tore
The shrieking wretch, who strove in vain
With one long hand to grasp his mane.
Eluding each dire stretch and strain,
The taunting fiend, with hellish pain
  His whilom master wore.
And now the spray mists intervene
A welcome veil across the scene;
And now they break—the cliff is clean.
  That sight was seen no more.

And thus the region had relief;
Thus vanished from the wilds the Thief.
Never again on Thorsfjeld's crest
Did he appear, or sheep molest.

His staff, preserved by Ola Brand,
Was long the wonder of the land.
No human blacksmith forged the bar;
'Twas wrought beneath the earth afar.
If anyone save Brand alone
(Whose mastery now it seemed to own)
Did handle it, as men are prone,
It burned his fingers to the bone.
But greatest marvels pall at last,
And this strange relic of the past,

Of trows or elves the workmanship,
Was destined by ill chance to slip
From place of honor dismally;
For Ola fashioned it to be
A thing a menial place to fill—
The spindle of a water-mill!*
And thus it wore itself away
With groans and shrieks from day to day.
Sparks flew from underneath the mill;
In truth it served the purpose ill.

At length one night when winds were high,
And densest clouds obscured the sky;
When, swoln with melting snow and rain,
The burn of Shandrick rose amain,
Forth to the mill, through slush and mire,
With corn to grind, went Hakon Gyar.

Quick as the quern began to spin
Did ear-astounding screams begin.
Around the mill, above, below,
Wild yells of more than human woe.
Louder and louder waxed the cries;
The peasant's hair began to rise.
Now Hakon Gyar, though he did try
His own exploits to magnify,

---

* See Note V.

Was not faint-hearted, but to hear
That din was more than man could bear.
And so he was about to turn
The stream, and stop the uncanny quern,
When suddenly, with thunderous roar,
The mill-roof bodily uptore
From off the walls, and fled away;
And Gyar in utter darkness lay,
Crouched in a corner, stunned with fright,
Staring upon a fearsome sight.

For lo! the Sheep Thief's awful form,
Bright, mid the blackness of the storm,
Upon the flying mill-stone stood
And pointed to his ancient rod.
The flying mill-stone rent in two,
Into his hand the spindle flew,
And through the floor, in dark turmoil,
The waters break, and round them boil.
Wildly the shattered building sways;
It trembles, totters, to its base;
The walls bend inward. With a bound
Gyar cleared the door, and, well-nigh drowned,
He struggled to a knoll, which stood
An island in the raging flood.

Down went the mill, in ruin down ;

Above it foamed the waters brown,

And on the knoll, in mortal fear,

The peasant kept his vigil drear,

Till broke the gloomy morn at last,

And through the shallowing tide he passed,

Reaching his home ; but from that night

His form was bent, his hair was white.

NOTES TO THE SHEEP THIEF.

I.—Often a birdnester, hanging by a rope, will see a nest safe from his reach under a jutting crag. Sometimes, when the cliff has only a moderate projection, he overcomes the difficulty by bracing his feet against the face of the cliff and bounding outward. Being instantly let down from above, his inward sway tends to carry him under the crag to his object.

II.—"Tangie" was an evil spirit in the form of a black horse. If anyone mounted him, he would immediately go over the nearest cliff in a blue flame. He differed from ordinary ponies in having cloven hoofs.

III.—Each flock of "skarfs," or cormorants, has a sentinel or nightwatchman stationed a little apart from the rest ; and if he can be secured without noise, the others are an easy prey.

IV.—"Ponies staunch and strong." It is a well-known fact that a real old-fashioned Shetland pony will trot away easily and sure-footedly under a man as heavy as himself. He is also remarkably intelligent.

V.—"A water-mill." The Shetland grain mills are of very primitive construction, consisting merely of the two millstones and a horizontal wheel under the floor beneath them. This wheel and the upper stone are firmly connected by an iron rod, called a spindle, which passes through a hole in the nether millstone, consequently the wheel and the mill revolve at exactly the same rate of speed. Of course, such machinery requires a very strong force of water, and thus the mills are useless except when the streams are high. In fact, heavy rains are known in Shetland as "mill-waters."

There may be half a dozen of these structures, belonging to different hamlets, all within a mile's radius, and there are no millers, but each villager has the use of the mill on a certain day of the week, and grinds his own corn.